D1133057

Randall
and
Randall

by Nadine Poper   illustrations by Polina Gortman

foreword by Dr. John E. Randall
renowned ichthyologist emeritus, Bishop Museum, Honolulu

BLUE WHALE PRESS

To all: Be symbiotic no matter how annoying, because the oceans
are depending on us – N.P.

To "The Broad Strokes," who lift me up and support me
on this journey – P.G.

To Dr. John Randall, for his life's contributions to marine science.
Mahalo, Jack – BWP

Sand dollar

Plankton

Sea cucumber

Randall and Randall

Text copyright © 2019 by Nadine Poper
Illustrations copyright © 2019 by Polina Gortman
All rights reserved

Published by Blue Whale Press LLC, U.S.A.

The artwork for this book was drawn with dip pen and ink, painted in watercolor, and colored using pencil on paper before being digitally touched-up and assembled.

Visit us at www.bluewhalepress.com, or contact us by sending email to info@bluewhalepress.com

Address all inquiries to Blue Whale Press, 237 Rainbow Dr. #13702, Livingston, TX 77399

Publisher's Cataloging-in-Publication data available upon request

Library of Congress Control Number: 2019932896

ISBN: 978-0-9814938-7-9 (hardcover)
ISBN: 978-0-9814938-8-6 (paperback)

First Edition

I received a query from the author some time ago asking for information on the symbiotic association that exists between a pistol shrimp and a gobiid fish for a children's book she was writing. This seemed like an unusual request: *Why would anyone write a children's book on such a complex subject as symbiosis?* On second thought, maybe a children's book is the place to begin. In this example, the fish is a goby that lives in a burrow that is quarried and maintained by a pistol shrimp.

There are more species of gobies in the sea (and some in freshwater) than any other family of fishes, and they are well-represented in nearly every habitable marine environment—even on open stretches of sand or mud. On such bottoms, the goby needs a partner to create a burrow in which to hide. That partner is a pistol shrimp of the genus *Alpheus*, usually a male-female pair of shrimps. The shrimp does not have good vision compared to that of the goby. However, it has a long slender pair of antennae with which it can maintain contact with its goby partner when it leaves the burrow. It also has a pair of little claws called "chelipeds" with which it can grasp food or move small stones or pieces of shell with which it constructs an arch to keep the burrow entrance from collapsing. The shrimp also becomes a little bulldozer to move sediment away when it piles up outside the burrow entrance. If the sediment is excessive, it spins around and moves a series of muscular flaps called "swimmerets" that are located on the underside of the abdomen with such vigor that sediment is sent flying away.

You might ask, "What does the goby do to deserve such dedication by the shrimp to construct and maintain the place for it to sleep at night and escape to shelter when threatened during the day?" The goby is a sentinel. Not only does it have superior vision to see an approaching predator—whether fish, crustacean, or octopus—but it has a sense to detect an incoming wave from an onrushing predator, even before the predator can be seen. This is due to the many tiny hairs within sensory pores on the goby's head and along the lateral line on the side of the body that vibrate with the velocity of incoming sound, sending that message to its brain. The goby reacts to this vibration by flicking its caudal fin, which signals the shrimp to flee to the burrow. If the predator is very near, the goby spins around and forces the shrimp into the burrow before following it in.

Children's books can be simply entertaining, or like this one, they can be educational as well. Two books I read as a teenager were a major factor in my becoming a marine biologist: *Beneath Tropic Seas*, written by William Beebe; and *Sea of Cortez*, written by John Steinbeck and his close friend, the marine biologist Ed Ricketts. John Steinbeck visited me when I directed a marine biological survey of the Virgin Islands National Park on the island of St. John. I took him for his first scuba dive!

Jack

–Dr. John "Jack" Randall, Senior Ichthyologist Emeritus, Bishop Museum, Honolulu, Hawaii

In warm tropical waters off the coast of Mexico, a busy pistol shrimp bulldozed a burrow for himself.

"My name's Randall, too! What's that snapping sound?"

"My claw. The sound keeps predators away."

"Come on out a little farther, Randall."

"Are you *loco*? Something will eat me for sure! All day long, I am in and out of *mi casa* clearing the bits of shells and sand. I can barely see, and there are predators lurking about. I fear for my life."

"Tell you what ... an eel just chased me out of my coral home, and I need a place to live. How about I guard *our* burrow while you dig?

I know all about predators. If one comes near, I'll wiggle and flick my tail. You'll feel that movement with your antennae and know not to come out. You'll be safe with me."

"*¡Espléndido! Gracias,* Randall."

"You're welcome, Randall."

"But I like to sing. It makes me happy.

Tra-la-la! He says my singing is bad. That makes me kind of ma—

Holy Mackerel! Predators!"

"Plankton will not eat me.

Be on the lookout for something *más grande.*"

"Randall? Do you think you could be quiet out there? Digging is hard work, and your singing is distracting me."

"Well, Randall, guarding a burrow is also hard work. Singing helps me concentrate.

La-la-la! Guarding is hard work, and my friend is acting like a—

Uh-oh! Trouble!"

"What is near?"

"A sand dollar."

"A tiny sand dollar will not eat me. Watch for something bigger.

I thought you knew about predators." *SNAP! SNAP!*

flick

flick

flick

"Please stop snapping. I'm getting a headache."

"Your headache is from your singing, not from my snapping."

"Laaaa la laaaaa! Randall is not so sweet. I doubt anything will want to eat—
Uh-oh! Trouble!"

"What is near this time?" *SNAP! SNAP!*

"A sea cucumber, and it's BIG!"

"*Ay*, Randall. Yes, sea cucumbers are big. However, they will not eat me. They eat—"

"Cucumbers?"

"No, Randall. They eat poop! Poop from other ocean critters. And they eat plankton. You don't know anything about predators." *SNAP!*

"I do so! And stop making that snapping sound. It hurts my ears."

"I have to snap. It's what I do. I am a snapping pistol shrimp.

Do you even have ears?"

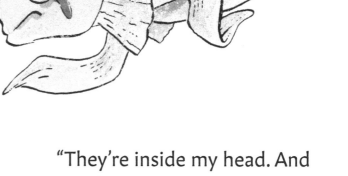

"They're inside my head. And they're beginning to ring from all your snapping!"

Randall hadn't gotten very far when
he saw something.

Something BIG.

Something DARK.

Something DANGEROUS.

SOMETHING...

"Don't be afraid, little goby. I have already eaten my lunch today . . . or have I?"

The shark inched forward. Randall inched backward.

"I-I-I saw a plump sea cucumber earlier. He would make a nice lunch for you, Mr. Shark. Mmmm . . . maybe dipped in some p-p-plankton?"

The shark swam closer.

Randall quivered, he wiggled, and he flicked.

Then all of a sudden, out of a batch of blue coral . . .

SNAP!
SNAP!
SNAP!
SNAP!
SNAP!
SNAP!
SNAP!
SNAP!
SNAP!
SNAP!

Later that night, in the warm waters off the coast of Mexico, Randall and Randall snuggled in their burrow.

"La-la-la, I have a friend under the sea, his snaps drove me crazy until he saved me. La-la-la-la-la-la-la-la—"

Randall! Could you please ...